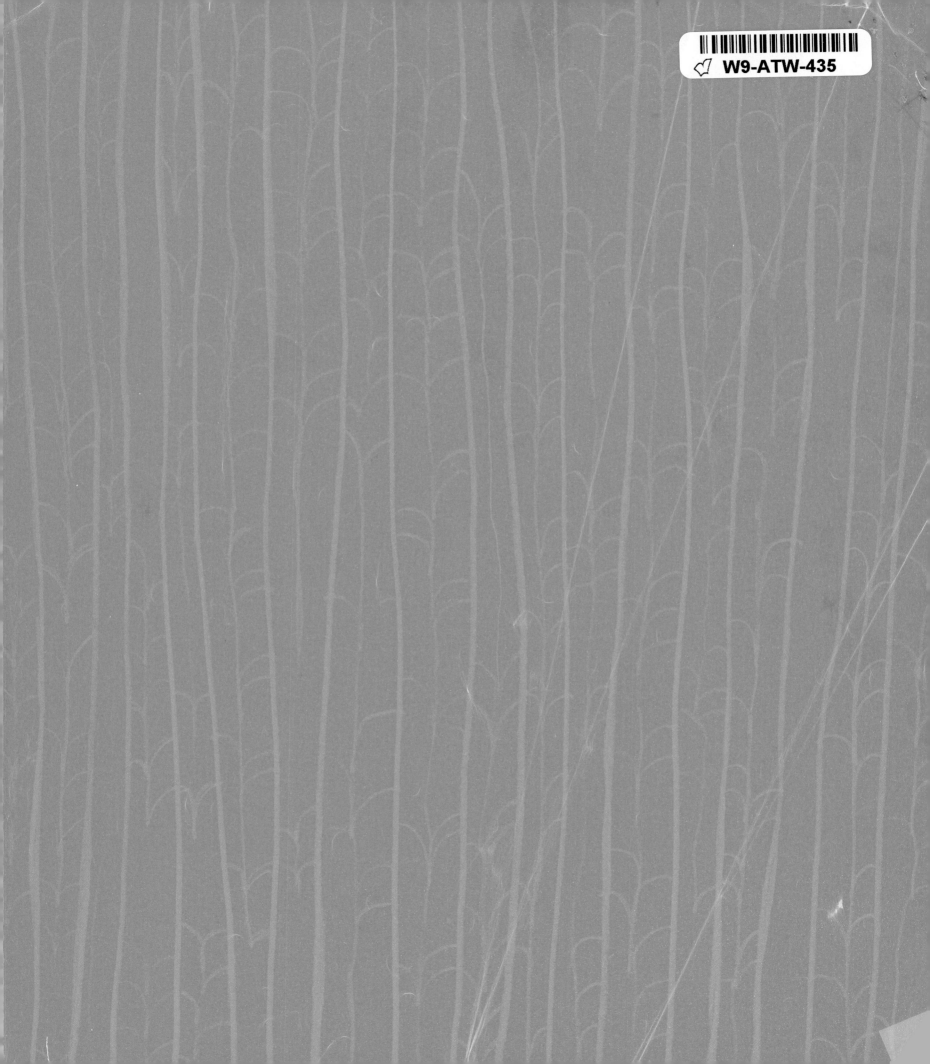

Ode to an Onion

story by
ALEXANDRIA GIARDINO

pictures by
FELICITA SALA

cameron kids

Photograph reprinted with permission from Archive Fundación Pablo Neruda.
English translation of "Oda a la cebolla" © 2018 by Alexandria Giardino.
Spanish poem "Oda a la cebolla," *Odas elementales* © 1954,
Pablo Neruda y Fundación Pablo Neruda.

Library of Congress Control Number
Catologing-in-Publication information available.
ISBN: 978-1-944903-34-3

Book design by Melissa Nelson Greenberg

Printed in China.

10 9 8 7 6 5 4 3 2 1

Cameron Kids is an imprint of CAMERON + COMPANY

CAMERON + COMPANY
Petaluma, California
www.cameronbooks.com

For Nicolas, whose energy and spirit are as big as Pablo's.
Gracias, mi hijo, por todo.

—A.G.

For James.

—F.S.

Pablo was hard at work,
writing a long, sad poem.
His pen whirled.
The pages piled high.

The clock struck twelve.

Pablo jumped. He was going to be late for lunch with his friend, Matilde. He combed his hair and wished he didn't look so gloomy.

Matilde liked to laugh.
She had a smile as wide as a guitar.
Pablo tried to hide his glum expression
behind a bouquet of poppies.

"No time for sadness," Matilde said
as she filled a vase with water.
"Come! I need your help with lunch."

Matilde led Pablo to where fennel grew
among tomato bushes. The air smelled like
licorice and mud.

"These plants are always getting tangled up with each other," Matilde said. She plucked a tomato.

"They must be fighting over who gets more sunshine," Pablo sighed.

"Oh no," Matilde laughed,
"they're just doing a tango."

Matilde headed to where the air smelled tangy and sweet.

"My garlic has fallen in love with
my roses," she said, harvesting a bulb.

Pablo shook his head. "How sad they have to separate."

"Oh, they'll meet again." Matilde snipped a bud.
"Now, for some onions."

Matilde strode to the peach tree.

"My onions grow here," she explained,
"because they want to protect the peaches."

"Their stalks do look like swords," Pablo said.
He watched Matilde pull a bulb from the dark earth.

"Thank you for taking care of the peaches,"
Matilde whispered to the onion. "Now,
I need you in my kitchen."

"Where it will only make you cry when
you slice it up." Pablo shrugged.

"My dear poet," Matilde said, "you are so glum today. All you see is sadness."

Pablo said, "My heart is heavy because I was writing a poem about poor miners who do very hard work."

Matilde put her arm through Pablo's.

"Their work is hard, but even miners must eat lunch," she said. "Come, I need you to slice the onion for our salad."

The onion's papery skin crinkled in Pablo's hand. As soon as he cut the onion, its earthy scent filled the air, making Pablo think of the garden, of the fennel struggling for sunlight, and the garlic longing for the roses. The scent burned Pablo's eyes. Tears streamed down his cheeks.

At first, all he saw through his tears was a lowly vegetable.

But then he noticed how the sunlight shone through the onion's layers.

"This onion came out of the dark earth," Pablo said,
"to shine like a bright moon."

"Aren't onions beautiful?" Matilde smiled.
"Wait 'til you taste it."

Pablo bit into a slice. First came sharpness, but then came sweetness. He offered Matilde a piece. "Thank you," he said, wiping away tears, "for reminding me that even though there is sadness in the world, there is so much happiness."

"Even in the simplest things," Matilde said, wiping away her own tears.

"Like onions," Pablo said.

"You should write about that!" Matilde laughed.

"Luminous onion," Pablo proclaimed, lifting the onion up high,
"sad things have always made me cry, but you have made me cry tears of joy!
For that, I will celebrate you as only a poet can. With an ode!"

"But first," Matilde said, "let's eat!"

About Pablo & Matilde

Pablo Neruda was born in Chile in 1904. He began writing poetry when he was a young boy, and at the age of nineteen, he became famous for a book of love poems. Because Pablo was a sensitive person who noticed injustices everywhere, he used the power of his poems to describe what he saw, hoping his readers would be touched and want to make the world a better place. After publishing many books of elevated poems, Pablo began writing simple odes because he wanted to write about common, everyday, and happy things, like socks and soup. Around this time, he met Matilde Urrutia at a concert in a park in Santiago, Chile. Matilde was a folk singer who laughed easily and often. Pablo reveled in her lighthearted spirit, and they fell in love. They built a home together, where Matilde kept an abundant garden and Pablo worked at a driftwood table, writing odes about everything from corn to artichokes and, yes, even onions!

Among Pablo's most celebrated works are *Selected Odes*, *Canto General*, and *Twenty Love Poems and a Song of Despair*. He also wrote a memoir called *I Confess I Have Lived*. This story, *Ode to an Onion,* was inspired by Pablo's poem "Oda a la Cebolla" and Matilde's memoirs, *My Life with Pablo Neruda*.

Ode to the Onion

by Pablo Neruda
Translated by Alexandria Giardino

Onion,
luminous vessel,
petal by petal
your beauty formed,
scales of glass made you swell,
and in the secrecy of the dark earth
your womb grew round with dew.
Beneath the earth
the miracle happened,
and when your clumsy green sprout
appeared
and your blades like swords
were born in the garden,
the earth amassed her power
bringing forth your naked transparency,
and as in Aphrodite's birth, the remote sea
reproduced the magnolia
raising up its bosom,
like that the earth
made you,
onion,
bright as a planet,
and destined
to shine,
constant constellation,
round rose of water,
upon
the dining table
of the poor.

Generous you
undo
your globe of freshness
in the fervent consummation
of the pot,
and in the fiery heat of the oil
a sliver of glass
becomes a curled feather of gold.

I shall also recall how fertile
your influence was on the salad's love,
and the heavens seem to conspire,
giving you the fine shape of hail
to celebrate your sharp sting
upon the hemispheres of a tomato.
But within the reach
of the people's hands,
showered with oil,
sprinkled
with a little salt
you vanquish the hunger
of the laborer along the hard road.
Poor people's star,
fairy godmother
wrapped
in delicate
paper, you arise from soil
eternal, intact, pure
like the seed of a star,
and upon cutting you
the kitchen knife
draws forth the only
sorrowless tear.
You made us cry without hurting us.
I have sung the praises of everything, onion,
but to me you are
more beautiful than a bird
of dazzling feathers,
in my eyes you are
heavenly globe, platinum goblet,
motionless dance
of the snowy sea anemone

and the scent of the earth lives
in your translucent nature.

Translated with permission from
the Fundación Pablo Neruda.

Oda a la Cebolla

by Pablo Neruda

Cebolla,
luminosa redoma,
pétalo a pétalo
se formó tu hermosura,
escamas de cristal te acrecentaron
y en el secreto de la tierra oscura
se redondeó tu vientre de rocío.
Bajo la tierra
fue el milagro
y cuando apareció
tu torpe tallo verde,
y nacieron
tus hojas como espadas en el huerto,
la tierra acumuló su poderío
mostrando tu desnuda transparencia,
y como en Afrodita el mar remoto
duplicó la magnolia
levantando sus senos,
la tierra
así te hizo,
cebolla,
clara como un planeta,
y destinada
a relucir,
constelación constante,
redonda rosa de agua,
sobre
la mesa
de las pobres gentes.

Generosa
deshaces
tu globo de frescura
en la consumación
ferviente de la olla,
y el jirón de cristal
al calor encendido del aceite
se transforma en rizada pluma de oro.

También recordaré cómo fecunda
tu influencia el amor de la ensalada,
y parece que el cielo contribuye
dándote fina forma de granizo
a celebrar tu claridad picada
sobre los hemisferios de un tomate.
Pero al alcance
de las manos del pueblo,
regada con aceite,
espolvoreada
con un poco de sal,
matas el hambre
del jornalero en el duro camino.
Estrella de los pobres,
hada madrina
envuelta
en delicado
papel, sales del suelo,
eterna, intacta, pura
como semilla de astro,
y al cortarte
el cuchillo en la cocina
sube la única lágrima
sin pena.
Nos hiciste llorar sin afligirnos.
Yo cuanto existe celebré, cebolla,
pero para mí eres
más hermosa que un ave
de plumas cegadoras,
eres para mis ojos
globo celeste, copa de platino,
baile inmóvil
de anémona nevada

y vive la fragancia de la tierra
en tu naturaleza cristalina.

——————————————